HI, CAT!

EZRA JACK KEATS

ALADDIN BOOKS
MACMILLAN PUBLISHING COMPANY
NEW YORK

Library of Congress Cataloging-in-Publication Data. Keats, Ezra Jack. Hi, cat!   Summary: Archie's day would have been great if he had not started it by greeting the new cat on the block.   [1. Cats—Fiction.   2. Afro-Americans—Fiction]   I. Title.   PZ7.K2253Hi   1988   [E]   87-37433
ISBN 0-689-71258-8

10   9   8   7   6   5   4   3

For David Hautzig

On his way to meet Peter,
Archie saw someone new on the block.

"Hi, cat," he said as he walked by.

He looked at his reflection in a store window.

Peter was waiting at the corner.
"Make way for your ol' gran'pa,"
Archie said in a shaky voice.
He looked Peter up and down.
"My, my, Peter, how you've grown!"

Why, gran'pa," Peter said.
It's good to see you."
Hello, my children," Archie croaked.
Hi, gran'pa!" Susy giggled.

Willie was so happy to see Archie
he ran over and licked his face.
Archie tasted delicious!
Willie licked and licked and licked.

"No respect for old age!"

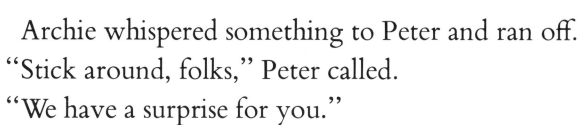

Archie whispered something to Peter and ran off.
"Stick around, folks," Peter called.
"We have a surprise for you."

When Archie got back,
he and Peter worked
while everyone waited.

"OK!" Peter announced.
"Make way for Mister Big Face!"
  A big paper bag appeared.
  Then a tongue stuck out of one of the eyes!

A hand came out of an ear
and motioned everyone to move closer.
They all obeyed.

Suddenly the bag began to shake.

It shook harder, and harder, and—

MEEOOW!

People started to leave.

"Wait—wait—the show'll go on!
See the tallest dog in the world
take a walk!" Archie shouted.

"Some show, gran'pa!"

"Some tall dog!"

"Who ate your mustache, gran'pa?"

Everyone walked away, laughing.

Soon no one was left except Archie, Peter,

Willie and the torn paper bag.

"It would have been great
    if it wasn't for that crazy cat," said Peter
as they walked home.
"Mmmm," said Archie. "He sure stuck around."

". . . and all I said was 'Hi, cat,' " said Archie,
   finishing his story.
"You're well rid of a cat like that,"
   said his mother.
   Archie thought for a while.
"You know what, Ma?" he said.
"I think that cat just kinda liked me!"